Also by Dean Marney:

The Easter Bunny That Ate My Sister
The Turkey That Ate My Father
The Jack-O'-Lantern That Ate My Brother
The Christmas Tree That Ate My Mother
Dirty Socks Don't Win Games
The Computer That Ate My Brother

DEAN MARNEY

SCHOLASTIC INC.
New York Toronto London Auckland Sydney

No part of this publication may be reproduced in whole or in part, or stored in a retrieval system, or transmitted in any form or by any means, electronic, mechanical, photocopying, recording, or otherwise, without written permission of the publisher. For information regarding permission, write to Scholastic Inc., 555 Broadway, New York, NY 10012.

ISBN 5-590-98830-1

Copyright © 1997 by Dean Marney. All rights reserved. Published by Scholastic Inc. APPLE PAPERBACKS and the APPLE PAPERBACKS logo are registered and/or registered trademarks of Scholastic Inc.

12 11 10 9 8 7 6 5 4 3 2 1   7 8 9/9 0 1 2/0

Printed in the U.S.A.   40

First Scholastic printing, March 1997

For Blythe, Dylan, and Luke

1

When the wizards came it was summertime. I didn't know anything about wizards except that they are mysterious. It should've been a great summer. It was supposed to be a great summer.

It was hot from the very start when school got out. People said we were having a drought. It was hot as anything during the day and then at night we had electrical storms but no rain. Have you ever seen ball lightning?

We were fishing on the river when I was littler and my mom kept saying, "Let's go. Look at those mean-looking clouds! It's going to rain and we'll probably get struck by lightning and die."

My dad said, "We'll go soon."

He didn't want to leave because the fish were finally starting to bite and we'd already fished for over an hour without a nibble. My mom put her pole away and started packing up the stuff. She had just told my older brother Alex to pick up his lunch garbage, when we heard a loud "pop."

It sounded like a giant balloon being popped and then I saw this big ball of light come flying down the river. At first I thought it was the end of the world and then I thought it was a UFO. It just appeared and was gone before you could count to three.

My dad said, "You just saw ball lightning. Have you ever seen it before?"

"No," I said with my mouth hanging wide open.

Alex said, "Cool." He wanted to wait around and see if it would happen again.

My mother said, "No way."

We got into the car and I said, "That was amazing."

"You're right there," said my dad.

I couldn't wait to get home and look it up in the encyclopedia. I look everything up in the encyclopedia. I have two complete sets and one not-so-complete set. I'm collecting them. I buy them at garage sales with my mom. She must go to at least one garage sale a day, most days two.

One set, the people just gave to me so they could get rid of it. I hauled it home in an old baby buggy my mom had bought at another garbage sale. The sets are all old but they're still good for looking up things like lightning.

Anyway, I looked up lightning and it said that

ball lightning was all this stuff about electricity and atoms and stuff. They said it was usually the size of a grapefruit. I don't think so. I thought maybe they'd never seen it before. I had the feeling that whoever wrote the article knew a ton of scientific things about ball lightning but they didn't really get it. It was something scary, truly amazing, and mysterious. They should've said that. That's all I should really say about my experience with wizards, they're scary, truly amazing, and mysterious.

That summer, right after school had quit for the year, I'd played all day and gone to bed quite late. I was lying in bed and it was hot but there was a breeze. There was a thunder and lightning storm that was keeping me awake. It would flash and I would count till it thundered so I knew how many miles away it was. I was only getting to about three.

I finally got up and went over to my window. I didn't just see some lightning. There were lights on in the haunted house next door, which is the biggest and the oldest and the strangest on the block. No one ever lives there very long. Some people say it's a haunted house. My dad says it was just poorly built. All I know is that it is very big and very old and very rickety and might as well be haunted. Anyway, there was a flash of lightning and the whole sky lit up and I saw what looked like someone moving stuff into the house. I grabbed my binoculars. A man in black robes was carrying some huge boxes into the house.

Have you ever seen someone and known something about him even though you haven't even met him yet? That happens to me all the time. Something inside me was saying, "He's a wizard." I got a chill.

I looked at the clock. It was just after midnight. I thought at the time you'd have to be strange to move into a house in the middle of the night. I was right.

2

Wizards are so mysterious they aren't even in my encyclopedias. I looked twice. I watched the man I knew was a wizard move into the house until I couldn't hold my eyes open any longer. I realize he could've been a vampire or a teacher or anything else, but I knew he was a wizard. What I'm not sure of is whether he knew I was watching him. He looked up toward our house and my window once but it was dark, I was behind my ugly curtains, and he was too far away. He couldn't have seen me but it felt like he did.

Now how did I know he was a wizard? I don't understand it myself. I've always been able to know things about people before they tell me. My mother says it is a gift called "intuition." My father says it's a curse. I've never really cared.

Maybe you can't tell things about me without me telling you, so I should probably tell you my name. I suppose you've guessed I'm a girl but maybe you haven't. It probably doesn't matter anyway unless we're going to get married or something. My name is Becky and I'm quiet. I'm really not that quiet but I am quieter than most kids. I like to listen and watch things and people. You can't do that when you're making noise all the time.

Sometimes my being quiet and watching and listening makes people nervous. They think I'm up to something. Well, sometimes I am and sometimes I'm not. It all depends.

I'm eleven years old since January 12th. I baked my own birthday cake because I thought it would be fun. I made it to look like a small volcano. I put a paper cup of dry ice in the volcano so it looked like it was smoking. It was pretty cool-looking. It didn't taste too good because I had to use so much frosting to make the lava. I don't like really sweet stuff that much.

I like animals best. If I had to decide between animals and people, I would take animals. One thing I like about them is they're most of the time quiet like me unless someone is riling them up. My dog Irving is a beagle and he'll watch me for hours without saying a word. However, he isn't always quiet. If there's a full moon you can hardly do a thing to keep him from baying at it for at least a little bit.

I used to think I'd like to bay at the moon. I figured it wasn't very ladylike although I know some ladies who could bay at the moon quite nicely. I guess I'm just not the type.

At our school, there are two types of girls. There are Barbies, who are the girls who care about clothes and are crazy about boys and what boy likes what girl. And there are Toms. Toms are the tomboys who play baseball and soccer with the boys and don't care much if their hair looks all that nice.

I'm neither a Tom or a Barbie. I'm a Becky. I'd rather weigh three hundred pounds and not be able to get through the door than be a Barbie. I'm probably closer to being a Tom, but it is just because my friend Jeff makes me play sports and stuff with him.

Jeff has been my friend forever. I'm not quiet around him. He lives two houses down. He's my age and goes to my school. We've been in the same class since first grade.

Jeff likes the Barbies. He probably wants to marry one or at least borrow her sports car when he grows up. I wouldn't want him for a boyfriend anyway.

That summer we were going to do summer swim team together. Neither one of us is fast at all, but you get to swim in the town pool when the other kids don't, like in the morning and late at night. You also get to have parties after the swim meets which is fun.

Jeff is smarter at some things than I am but he can't sit still. He'd rather be out playing some sport than sitting all day doing school stuff. Our teacher last year said he had problems concentrating in class and she tried to convince his mom that something was wrong with him. There is nothing wrong with him. He just cares more about basketball than he does about topographical maps.

Jeff likes animals, too. He doesn't have a dog so he borrows Irving. I let him. Irving doesn't mind. He likes Jeff.

Jeff has a fish tank with a big old catfish in it named Tim. It is kind of gross if you ask me. I don't ever borrow Tim. In fact, I keep telling him he should let it go but he won't because he can't stand the thought of someone catching Tim and eating him.

Jeff and his mom live with his grandparents. His parents have split up. His dad is in Alaska, but he comes home to see Jeff sometimes.

Jeff looks forward to the day he can go visit his dad in Alaska. His dad tells him he can do it when he's older. However, he never tells him how much older he has to be.

I don't really like Jeff's dad and I don't even know him. Luckily my dad is around. Jeff likes my dad. He even likes my older brother Alex.

Alex is fifteen and has several screws loose. He has a gorilla suit that my mom picked up at a garage sale for him to wear for Halloween but instead he puts it on whenever he feels like it. He started out just wearing it in his room and then he watched TV in it and then he was wearing it all the time. In the summer it is especially weird because you know he is just sweating like a pig underneath it.

I heard him tell my mother, "I feel good when I'm a gorilla."

"Well you aren't a gorilla," my mother said. "I wish I'd never bought the darn thing."

That is what she said, but she never made him get rid of it. She told everyone it was just a phase. Her sister thought it was weird and told her so. However, she's also told my mom that she can read a person's future by looking at the position of the moles on their arms and the pimples on their faces, so I guess she doesn't have much room to talk.

I don't really know why Alex has to wear a gorilla suit but I figure that it doesn't really hurt anything. It makes Irving bark but that's about it. The neighbors think it's a little odd but they all do something odd in their own way.

Alex was supposed to paint the outside of the house for the last three summers. He kept trying to get out of it. Seems like there was always a reason. He had to go someplace or do something or he didn't want to get paint on his gorilla suit. Our house has needed painting a long time. I guess it likes it that way. But it still looks better than the house next door.

3

It had been a couple of weeks after I had seen the wizard in black moving in next door. No one else had seen anything human go in or come out of the haunted house since. They did notice that the huge yard around the house was starting to look a whole lot better. The trees we thought looked dead were sprouting leaves and the grass started to green up and grow. There were even flowers blooming. Mysteriously, all this was happening without anyone ever seeing someone working in the yard or watering or anything. The second thing that got noticed was that someone had chained a big old Doberman to the front door and he barked and scared the bejeebers right out of you even if you walked by on the opposite side of the street.

You can usually make friends with most animals, you just have to know how. You have to take your time and be careful. But I didn't think I could ever get close enough to that monster to make friends. He was the meanest slobber-dripping dog you've ever seen. He had teeth like a Tyrannosaurus rex. I'd likely lose an arm or two before we would be pals.

Jeff said, "If you could get close enough to him to get a saddle on, you could ride him."

We were sitting out on my porch on the sofa that we'd just moved out of the living room to make room for the new one my mother bought at a garage sale that afternoon. My parents had to go and pick it up after dinner and my dad was mad.

"We don't need a couch," he said.

"Well," my mom replied, "it will look just perfect in the living room. You'll see."

"And," Dad added, "the one on the porch looks fine, too. It will probably stay there forever because I'm not moving it."

"That's all right," she whispered to me. "I'll put an ad in the paper and we'll sell it in a week tops."

She was wrong. It stayed there all summer till we finally hauled it to the Salvation Army. Jeff said that his grandma said it made us look like we lived in a trailer park. But I kind of liked having a couch on the porch. It was a comfortable place to sit. Irving liked it, too. He had never been allowed to sit on it in the house, although he'd sneak on when no one was looking. Out on the porch no one cared, so he'd stretch out like it was his.

We were sitting out on the porch just enjoying the evening and mostly watching the Doberman lunge and snap his chain at everyone who went by in a car, bike, or whatever.

"I hope the chain doesn't break," said Jeff.

Right then, Irving, who had his head in my lap, jumped up and started baying like crazy.

"What is with him?" Jeff asked.

"Irving be quiet!" I said.

He wouldn't stop.

"Tell that dog to keep quiet," my mom yelled from inside the house.

Then Irving ran off the porch over to the fence between our house and the haunted house. He stopped dead in his tracks and started growling. I don't think I'd ever heard him growl like that.

"What is wrong with him?" Jeff asked again. "He's freaking me out."

Jeff and I jumped down to where Irving was.

"What is it Irving? Come here," I said.

My dog wouldn't budge. He just stood there growling at the fence. I was starting to worry that the Doberman had gotten loose because I couldn't hear him or see him.

"Do you suppose your brother has his suit on around here somewhere?" asked Jeff.

"No," I said, "there's something else there."

I got between Irving and the fence, which is just a rickety old wire fence overgrown with grass and weeds and bushes. I looked over it. I couldn't see anything. Irving was still growling. He was going to give himself a sore throat.

12

I turned around and faced Irving and Jeff.

"Irving," I said, "knock it off or you have to go inside."

I looked at Jeff and he had the strangest look on his face. I guessed if someone saw a ghost he'd look just like Jeff did now. He looked like he couldn't talk and if he could talk he wouldn't know what to say. He was staring over the top of my head.

I turned around to see what was wrong, and then I jumped back and screamed.

"You scared the pants off me," I apologized to an old man dressed in a shiny green and gold bathrobe. He had a pointy hat with the same pattern as the bathrobe and he had long white hair and a beard. He certainly looked like a wizard should. "Where'd you come from?"

"You're all right now," he said, looking at Irving, and Irving just shut up and went back to lying on the couch.

"He doesn't usually growl," I said quietly. "He isn't mean."

"I like pets," nodded the wizard in agreement. "I have some unusual ones myself."

"I see your dog all the time," I said. "What's his name?" I nodded my head toward the haunted house's front porch.

"Oh, you mean the Doberman? He's nameless to me, unfortunately."

I heard an owl hooting.

"It's a nice night," I said, changing the subject. "My name's Becky and I'm your neighbor. This is my friend Jeff."

"It's a perfect evening for helping things grow," my neighbor said. "I'm talking to things. It makes them grow faster." Then he added something that bothered me. "You know what I am, don't you?"

I nodded like a dumb robot.

Then he said, "Trust what you know. You don't scare easily, do you?"

I didn't have a clue as to what I was supposed to say. He was talking about my not being scared and he'd just scared me. Then he raised his hands with the palms toward us and muttered something. And, without ever introducing himself, he simply smiled and turned and walked away.

"You can close your mouth now," I told Jeff after he'd left.

"He wasn't there and then he was."

"What are you talking about?" I asked.

"I was standing there watching you and you turned around and he just appeared. He didn't walk up or anything," Jeff said, waving his arms like he was trying to get the attention of a small airplane in the sky. "He was just there."

"That's crazy," I told him.

"Uh-huh," said Jeff, "it's scary. Maybe he's a ghost."

"He's probably a wizard," I countered.

"No way," said Jeff. "Is he?"

14

"What about that outfit?" I said. "Who would wear a get-up like that if you weren't a wizard?"

"Your brother would," suggested Jeff.

"I will ignore that because it was cruel and vicious," I informed him.

"He kind of freaked me out," Jeff said.

"What do you mean? He seemed nice enough."

"You're kidding, aren't you?"

"No," I answered.

"Is this the guy you saw move in?" quizzed Jeff.

"No, I guess there must be at least two of them," I said.

"I'm going home and I'm never going to see you again till they move, which will probably be tomorrow," Jeff joked.

"He *was* helping things grow," I mumbled under my breath.

4

I went into the house and my mother asked, "What happened to Jeff? Did he run off mad?"

"Nope," I said, "he just wanted to get home before it got too dark."

"Is that so?"

"Did I tell you our new neighbors are wizards and I just met one face-to-face?" I said.

My mother probably wasn't listening to exactly what I said. So, she answered, "Well, we will have to be neighborly won't we, although that dog is sure something."

How do you be neighborly to a wizard? I would've asked her but she had called her sister and was now concentrating on making bread-and-butter pickles and talking on the phone at the same time. They were talking about how they never get to take vacations.

That night, I thought I was dreaming about a sound. I heard this hissing noise. It sounded like air coming out of a big hose, but it didn't sound like

16

a machine. It sounded uneven as if something alive and big was taking in a huge amount of air and then letting it out with a hiss. I woke myself up.

Then I realized I wasn't dreaming. I could still hear it. At first I thought it was inside my room. I went to the window and I could hear the sound coming from the house next door but it was more like it was vibrating through the ground from the haunted house and up through our basement. There was something hissing like crazy, like a low-pitched tea kettle. I didn't like it. And it wouldn't stop. I also thought I heard a man laughing. I could hardly get back to sleep. I had to put the pillows over my ears.

The next morning I asked my mother if she had heard anything in the night.

"Just your father snoring loud enough to rattle the windows. If you heard anything, it was probably that."

"Does he hiss when he snores?" I asked.

"I don't think so," said my mom. Luckily my dad was already at work. I wouldn't have wanted to hurt his feelings.

My brother came to breakfast with his gorilla suit on. I didn't say a darn thing.

"Good grief," my mother remarked, "do you have to wear that flea-bitten thing to breakfast? I swear I'm throwing it away. At least wash the silly thing. It's starting to smell. And take off the head or you aren't eating anything."

17

He slowly took off his head. His hair was already sweaty and the day had just started.

"At least let me cut off the legs so it's cooler," said my mom.

"No way," said Alex.

"You have to paint today," demanded my mother. "You want cereal and toast?"

Alex just grunted at her.

"Alex, sweetheart, you know I love you, but you are trying the little ounce of patience that God had the grace to give me. I'm trying to be understanding of this gorilla phase but you have to help me by at least being civil."

He looked at her with his greasy hair and pimples, nodded his head, and said, "Okay."

"That's my boy," said Mom. "How about we get Becky here to help you slap some paint on this old place?"

"I hate to paint and I'm going to be busy trying to find out what was hissing all night long," I said.

"You heard that?" said Alex.

"Did you?" I asked.

"Maybe," he said, doing his best to ignore me.

"Just do a little bit, both of you," my mom said. "Becky, you can paint our house on the neighbor's side and that way you can watch if they come out. How about I bake some cookies? Except it is going to be too hot to use the oven. I know, I'll bake my chocolate No Bake Cookies and you can take some over to our new neighbors for us."

Sounds pretty good doesn't it? I like those cookies. I can even make them and I'm not much of a cook. (You can try making them yourself. The recipe's on page 105.)

My mom started making cookies and I went outside to help Alex paint.

"Where do you want me to start?" I asked. Irving had brought me a tennis ball he wanted me to throw. "Can't," I said to him.

Alex had taken off his gorilla suit and was in his painting shirt and some old shorts.

"I don't care," he said, taking his anger out on me. "You have to clean out your own brush and put away your own paint can."

He got out a paint can for me, shook it up, opened it, and handed me a brush. He then went onto the porch and sat on the couch, I guess to rest.

I started to tell him I wasn't going to help him if he was just going to sit around but the oddest thing happened. For no apparent reason, the hair on the back of my neck was standing up. The other thing was that I was suddenly cold but it was already eighty-five degrees out and climbing.

I couldn't move for a second and then something in me made me look over at the house next door. I couldn't see anything or anyone but I knew someone was watching me.

19

5

Later that afternoon, when I wouldn't do it, my mother carted a plate of those cookies over to the wizard next door.

"I'm sorry," I explained. "I've got paint all over me." The truth was I felt a little shy and uncomfortable and scared.

My mother looked at me like I was being lazy but she had also told me a million times to be wary of total strangers (and even people I knew) who acted strange.

"Well," she said, "I guess I can do it."

With that she marched over. She opened up the front gate to the haunted house and walked a good ways up the walk. The Doberman was hiding in the bushes waiting for her. He let her get almost too close and then he lunged at her, only stopping because he hit the end of his chain. My mother dropped the plate of cookies and hightailed it back home.

"Some people just don't care to be friendly," she said.

I guess it didn't scar her emotionally. She could make more cookies and she used a paper plate. She stood back and looked over where we had been painting.

"Good heavens," she exclaimed.

I thought we had done something terrible. Alex sat up. He had been lying down in the shade. I could see and hear the Doberman chomping on those cookies. I half hoped they would make him sick.

"Will you look at that clematis?" she said.

My mother loves clematis. It is a flowering vine that she could never really get to grow very well. I looked with her in shock.

"When did that happen?" I asked.

The clematis had grown and practically covered the side of the house where we had just been painting.

Alex looked at my mom. "What did you use for fertilizer?"

"I don't know what to say," said my mother, waving her arms and pointing at all the purple blossoms. "I've never had a green thumb, my sister has the green thumb, but look at this."

I don't know. I think she should have been more shocked and concerned. Something mysterious was going on and she was all excited that one of her plants had finally grown.

"I have a prize clematis," she said repeatedly as she walked into the house.

I next heard her on the telephone with her sister saying, "You won't believe this."

I felt someone staring at the back of my head. I whipped around and looked over at the haunted house next door. I couldn't see anyone.

With the hair still standing on the back of my neck, I walked slowly to our front door. I saw that our geraniums in the clay pots on the porch looked much bigger than I remembered earlier that morning. Our lawn also needed mowing, but then I remembered that my dad had just mowed it yesterday.

I had a feeling something was wrong. I realized I hadn't seen Irving for awhile. I called for him. Nothing. I then hollered in the house for him.

My mom said, "Hush honey, I'm talking to my sister."

"Have you seen Irving?" I said getting worried.

She motioned with her hand for me to leave the room. I went to find Alex. He was putting his gorilla suit back on.

"Have you seen Irving?" I said.

"Doberman probably ate him."

"That's not funny," I said quietly because that was exactly what I feared.

I went downstairs and into the backyard. I looked around and then started to go out to the front of the house to check up the street. I was hoping that maybe Jeff had borrowed him. I turned the corner of the house and I saw Irving. At first I was relieved and then I was slightly taken aback. He was standing perfectly still on three legs with the fourth tucked under him. He was facing away from me in the middle of the petunia bed that seemed to have recently grown to be the prettiest and biggest petunias you've ever laid eyes on.

"Irving," I called, "get out of the flower bed. Mom is going to kill you."

Irving didn't budge. I went over to him, reached down, touched him, and let out a scream like I had died because I could have.

The next thing I knew I was being carried by Alex in his gorilla suit. He plopped me down on the couch on the porch and yelled for Mom to bring me a glass of water.

"What happened?" I demanded.

"You must have fainted from the paint fumes and the heat," he said.

Then I remembered Irving.

I started bawling like I wouldn't ever quit. I tried to get up but Alex pushed me back down.

"I've got to get Irving," I blubbered.

Then my mother came out of the house.

"What's all the excitement?" she blurted out.

"She fainted," said Alex.

"Honey," she said, "do you need a doctor?"

"No, Irving," I said still crying.

"What about Irving?" she said. "You're delirious, you're not making sense."

"Irving is . . ." and I couldn't really say the final word, dead.

"Well Irving is right over there in . . . my gorgeous . . . absolutely huge . . . petunias! Irving you get out of there right now and I mean right now. Will you look at the size of those things?"

He didn't budge.

"Alex," she said, "go get Irving and bring him here."

Alex said, "He doesn't like my suit."

"Honey," she said, "the suit is becoming an irritant to all of us. Please take it off and go get Irving out of the petunias before your sister dies from a heatstroke and I have a nervous breakdown."

Alex, still in his gorilla suit, went over to Irving, picked him up like an old piece of furniture, and hauled him over to us.

"As you'll notice, this isn't Irving but I have to admit it looks an awful lot like him," said Alex bluntly.

I reached out and touched what was a perfect replica of my dog Irving, now made of plastic. He looked like one of those pink flamingo lawn ornaments except he was a beagle lawn ornament.

"Well," my mom sighed, "that almost beats the clematis for amazing, now doesn't it?"

6

The phone rang. My mother dropped Irving to the floor like a piece of trash and ran into the house to answer it.

"Is she weirder or is it just me?" asked Alex.

I couldn't answer his question. If you can't say something nice, you shouldn't say anything at all. I was staring at the plastic Irving. My mom came back out.

"It was just your friend," my mom said. "I told him you'd had a heatstroke and he's coming over. He asked if you were going to die."

"Jeff?" I said.

Out of the blue, my mother started laughing hysterically. Then she picked up Irving and started dancing around the porch.

Alex whispered to me, "I should call someone. I think she's flipped."

I knew something was very wrong and I was confused by everything, the plants, Irving being missing, and my mother. Maybe she'd had a heatstroke. I thought about Irving again and wondered if maybe we'd all had a heatstroke and I started crying.

Alex looked at me and said, "Don't worry, maybe she's only half flipped out."

"She's not alone," I said, pointing to the haunted house. "What do you make of that?"

The wizard in black was in the front yard jumping up and down. He was doing a wild-man dance and yelling and pointing at, I think, the trees and all the plants. He looked pretty silly. Then he climbed onto the porch, cupped his hands around his mouth, and yelled some more. First he faced down the street and then up the street.

"What is he doing?!" exclaimed Alex — like he'd never done anything strange before.

"I believe," I said, "he's yelling at the plants."

"Weird," said Alex, satisfied with my explanation.

Jeff came running around the corner, tripped on something, and sailed through the air. He hit the sidewalk with both hands and scraped them good. He got up, inspected his palms, and looked back to see what he'd tripped on.

"Where did that root come from?" he said.

"What root?" I asked.

"The root," he said sharply, "that wasn't there yesterday or the day before or the day before that or the week before that or the month before that or the year before that."

"Irving is missing," I sniffed.

"So is Tim, my best fish, my only fish," said Jeff, now sounding like he might cry, too.

My mom quit dancing and said, "Who wants lemonade?"

No one said anything and if we did we would've had to be quick because she was in the house before you could say Abraham Lincoln twice.

"Tim is gone and someone left a plastic statue of him in his place. It's a perfect likeness, except he's floating at the top of the tank."

I pointed to the statue of Irving.

"What's going on?" asked Jeff, very alarmed. He loved Irving as much as I did.

"I don't know," I said, "but I have a sneaking hunch that those two living next door have something to do with it."

"Let's go get them," said Jeff, ready for a fight.

"And then what?" I said.

"Get our pets back," said Jeff.

"We don't know they took them, do we?"

"I guess not," agreed Jeff. "Well, I guess we better find out first."

Alex, now bored with us, said, "I think I'll go to my room now."

"Thanks for picking me up," I said.

"Man," said Jeff, "your grass is as bad as ours."

"What do you mean? Stuff at your house is growing, too?"

"It's growing like crazy. You can watch it grow,

it is growing so fast. I honestly thought I could hear the grass grow," said Alex.

He was right. I looked at the grass, which was now a foot high, and it actually shot up an inch. The blades were getting wider too.

We were still watching the grass grow with me still lying on the couch like I was sick, when a girl from our block named Brooke came up the porch steps. She was carrying another plastic replica animal. This one was a cat.

"Have you guys seen my cat?" she asked.

"What's its name?" asked Jeff.

"Pickles," said Brooke.

I knew that. Brooke and I used to be really good friends. However, I didn't know Brooke very well anymore. She had turned into a Barbie. Not that she looked like Barbie, no one looks like Barbie. Besides, you don't have to look like Barbie to be one. She just started acting like a Barbie.

"Have you always had that plastic one?" I asked.

"No," she said, "I found it on our driveway. It's funny, it looks just like Pickles."

"I haven't seen her," Jeff said.

"Me neither," I added.

"I guess I'll just keep looking," Brooke said and turned and left.

"Brooke," I yelled after her, "if you run into my dog Irving, send him home."

"Okay," she said. "Who has moved in next door?"

Jeff answered before I could, "Somebody who is doing some pretty weird things."

Brooke giggled nervously. "Should I ask them if they've seen my cat?"

We both pointed toward the Doberman but the funny thing was, he wasn't there. We could see the chain but no dog. Then I looked up. I don't know what made me do it, but something told me to look up.

Sure enough on the porch roof of the haunted house, I saw the Doberman walking around. He turned toward us and I swear I could see all his teeth showing and he was growling right at me.

"How did he get up there?" asked Jeff. "Flew?"

"Where did Brooke go?" I said. "She was just here. Where did she go?"

I ran off the porch and looked down the street. She wasn't there. She just vanished.

"Did you see where she went?" I asked Jeff, who had joined me.

"No," said Jeff. "I was busy looking at the dog."

"Oh no," I said, "she didn't."

She was walking through the gate to the haunted house. We both ran after her. By the time we got there, she was running up to the porch with her plastic cat. The Doberman was still on the roof looking like some hideous gargoyle. The front door was wide open.

"Brooke," I yelled, "no!"

She turned like she sort of heard me but then she turned back and walked right up to the house. We watched as she walked across the porch and into the house. The door quickly closed behind her and I thought I heard a muffled scream.

7

"**M**aybe we should go in after her," I said to Jeff. We'd opened the gate and started up the sidewalk to the house.

"We'll just ring the doorbell and ask to speak to Brooke," stated Jeff.

Right then the Doberman dove off the roof like an Olympic diver doing a swan dive and landed running toward us, without a chain.

"Oh my," I said, grabbing Jeff and running like I'd never run before back to the gate.

We got through the gate just in time to slam it in his face.

"Sorry," I said to the Doberman.

"Are you crazy?" said Jeff. "He was going to kill you."

"Well, sorry I said sorry," I barked at Jeff.

I guess I get cranky when I get scared. I've also noticed that it always seems like when things start going bad, you can always count on them getting worse. Take my mother for instance. She forgot to make lunch and dinner.

She was dancing around the front room when we came into the house and she didn't stop. I tried to tell her about Brooke and she didn't care. I tried to tell her I was calling the police and she didn't care. She only cared about dancing.

"Did I tell you that I always wanted to be a dancer?" she said to me.

We tried to call the police but when we dialed we could only hear static on the line.

"My dad will know what to do," I said confidently.

My dad came home and at first he was very surprised at the growing landscape of the neighborhood and then I told him about Irving and Brooke and the telephone and the odd behavior of my mother. But it wasn't long before he was acting just as odd. He was acting like he didn't hear a word I said. He started mowing the lawn but it clogged the mower as soon as he started it so he went to bed and I swear to you he never got back up, except once. He got up and rolled a TV into his room.

"I'm tired," is what he said.

It started to rain. The drought was over and our yard continued to grow. In fact, all the yards in our neighborhood were growing.

The next day, Jeff and I walked around in the rain, dazed. Yards now looked like rain forests with waist-high grass and giant flowers. There were vines climbing all over the houses. Our neighborhood was looking more and more like a jungle every minute. No one went to work or anywhere.

We spent the day just watching it rain and everything grow. Jeff went home and I went to bed not knowing what to expect in the morning. The next morning it was the same but more. I had to cut the vines in order to get out the front door. I went to see what everyone else was doing.

At first all the kids on the block liked our new neighborhood. It was kind of fun. We could have played hide-and-seek in broad daylight and all you had to do was stand in someone's yard and you would never be found. But everything started growing so much that by the afternoon the street and most of the sidewalks were covered. If you stood too long in one place, you couldn't find yourself. I got lost going to Jeff's house.

And everyone's pets were gone. In their place were plastic replica statues. It seemed like every house in the neighborhood used to have a pet of some kind but now there was only one house that did. It was the house next door to me.

The mail didn't come or the paper. They couldn't find our houses.

Jeff was beating back a rosebush with a stick, or something that looked sort of like a rosebush that was trying to grow around his leg.

"Jeff," I said, "something is very wrong. Something bad is happening and it has to do with that house and the wizards."

"The haunted house," he reminded me.

"Exactly," I said, "we have to get in there."

Right then another girl my age, Claudia, went by on the sidewalk or what was left of the sidewalk because of all the roots pushing the concrete up. She was dragging a plastic replica of her dog by its leash behind her and crying.

"Claudia," I yelled. "What's wrong?"

"I don't know," she said. "I just feel so sad."

"Where are you going?" I asked.

"I don't know," said Claudia.

We watched as she walked away through the tall grass.

"See," I said to Jeff, "have you ever seen Claudia cry?"

"Well," said Jeff.

"I think we'd better follow her," I said.

"Why?"

"I don't know," I said, "we just should."

"Whatever," said Jeff, "but we'd better hurry. I think she went through those trees that are where the street used to be. Hey, I hear there is a creek now flowing through the Greens' yard."

"What was that?" I said, pointing upward toward the treetops.

"I think," said Jeff, "that was your brother in his gorilla suit."

"No way," I said.

We were at the haunted house just in time to see Claudia making her way up the path to the front porch.

"Claudia," I yelled, "don't."

She turned and looked at me with her red puffy eyes and then entered some bushes. We couldn't see her anymore. To be totally honest, Jeff and I were too chicken to go get her and I'm not proud of it. We made our way through the substantial foliage back to my house not knowing what else to do.

"I don't understand anything," I said.

"It's a jungle out there," my dad said from upstairs.

8

That night it rained even harder. It seemed to go on forever. It rained solid, all night. It poured out of the sky like I never remember it raining. I sat in my room looking out through the tree branches that were now in front of my window, and I could barely see the haunted house next door.

Now, I could have been hallucinating, I can't tell for certain, but this is what I think I saw without my binoculars. I saw the wizard in the black robes standing on top of the roof holding a lightning rod, getting struck fifteen or twenty times and laughing his head off.

The next morning I was so down I didn't leave the house. It seemed like it was too much work to do anything or try to go anywhere and besides there was nowhere to go. I was glad when Jeff came over.

"Something followed me," he said.

"What do you mean?" I said.

"I mean, that something was following me. It is probably still out there." He pointed out the front door.

"Do you think it was another kid?"

"Hardly," he said, "it was breathing too heavy."

"Was it an adult?"

"No," he said, "it couldn't be an adult."

"I give up," I said.

"I think it was an animal of some kind. It was like it was stalking me."

"All the animals are gone," I said.

"This one isn't. Maybe it was that Doberman," he guessed.

"You suppose?" I said.

Then my mother came into the room.

"Hi kids," she said, dancing through. "This is my sunshine dance after the rain."

"That's lovely, Mom," I said.

"I brought you some tomatoes," said Jeff.

"Oh thank you," she said. "I'll now dance the tomato harvest dance."

She danced away into the kitchen.

"Listen," said Jeff to me in a whisper, "I've had a dream and it is scaring me."

You might as well get used to it. I have hunches about things and Jeff has dreams.

"What?" I said also in a whisper but who could hear you in the jungle?

"I dreamt I went through the door of the house next door and all I know is that there is something powerful there."

"Oh really?" I said sarcastically.

"Don't *you* be mean," he said.

"Sorry," I said.

I then told him what I had seen standing on the roof and that I didn't think it was a dream.

"He really is a wizard," said Jeff, "and he's put a spell on our whole neighborhood, maybe the whole world."

"Dead right," I agreed.

"I also dreamt that there was something in your basement behind the shelves in the pantry," said Jeff soberly.

"Like what?" I said.

"I don't know."

"Well you dreamt a headful, didn't you?" I said loudly.

"We should go check your basement," said Jeff.

I could tell he was serious about it and it was futile for me to just ignore him. I knew that he thought there was something in the basement and he wouldn't be all right till we checked it out. We went to the top of the stairs. It was black as coal down there.

"Flip on the lights," said Jeff.

"Can't," I said, "they stopped working."

"Ours, too," said Jeff.

"I'll go get some candles," I told him.

All I could find were candles left over from the holidays. I grabbed two angel candles from the Christmas box in the hallway closet, lit them, and headed down the stairs. I was a little scared because it was so dark and because it was damp and cool as a tomb. Still, I was slightly more curious than afraid.

I tripped on something at the bottom of the stairs. I looked down and it was Irving. Well, you know, the fake Irving.

"What is he doing down here?" I said, picking him up and putting him on the stairs.

We went to the pantry door.

"Are you sure you want to do this?" I asked.

"Yes," said Jeff emphatically. "I, well, we have to."

I opened the door and a rat ran out. It made me jump through the roof.

"Well there's an animal," I said.

"Keep going," Jeff said.

"I am," I said. "Just don't push."

We were in the pantry.

"It's this wall," said Jeff.

"There's nothing there but shelves," I said. "We ate all the food off of it."

"No," he said, "it's behind the shelves."

"Okay," I said, "hold my candle."

I handed my candle to him and started taking the shelves apart.

"I'll help," he said, putting the candles on the ground.

"Kind of you," I said, laughing.

"Thanks for doing this," he said. "I know most people think my dreams are crazy."

"Well, my dad used to say that most things were dreams at one time or another before they were real."

The candles were casting an eerie glow in the pantry. At one point a bunch of the shelving collapsed and I got the screaming meemies.

"Shhhhh!" said Jeff. "What's that sound?"

I listened hard and through the wallboards behind the shelves you could hear the hissing sound I'd heard right after the wizard had moved in.

9

I went and found a hammer and a crowbar off my dad's workbench. Both were starting to rust. The dampness had caused oxidation to occur and rust had formed. I just thought I'd throw that in. I'm not showing off.

I handed Jeff the hammer (although he was company so I should've given him the crowbar because it was the better tool).

"Sorry," I said to him. "I have this thing for crowbars and I've always wanted to do this."

I took the crowbar and pried off a huge plank of wood. The hiss was immediately louder and a gust of wind coming from the blackness behind the boards blew our candles out.

"Jeff?" I said through the dark.

"What?" he said, lighting a match.

We relit the candles.

"It is better to light one little candle than to stumble in the dark," I recited, adding, "my grandma always said that."

We put our angels behind some empty jelly jars so we didn't have to protect them the whole time.

"I want to try the crowbar," said Jeff.

I was a little reluctant, but gave in. He removed another board and the hissing stopped. There was now a hole big enough for us to walk through.

"What do you suppose it is?" I asked.

"I suppose we should find out," said Jeff.

"Well, we could just say we found something and leave it at that," I suggested.

There was another long hiss and I thought I could hear kids' voices.

"We could do that," said Jeff, "but it sure looks like a tunnel to me and it goes someplace."

"Are you afraid?" I said.

"Ya," said Jeff. "Are you?"

"Uh-huh," I responded.

"A tunnel has to open up somewhere. Which way are we facing?" asked Jeff.

"I suppose," I said cautiously, "toward the haunted house next door."

"Do you think?" said Jeff.

"Maybe we should go get my dad," I said.

"You know he won't get out of bed," stated Jeff. It was the truth.

"I think we should think about safety," I demanded. "What if the whole thing caves in on us?"

"I think we're the last kids in the neighborhood left. We either go in there or they come and get us."

"Let them try," I said, grabbing the crowbar and holding it tightly.

"Have you seen any other kids in a couple of days?"

"I don't . . . remember," I stuttered. "Days blur, I can't tell who or what I've seen."

"But you've seen kids go into that house and not come back out?" reminded Jeff.

"Maybe," I said, knowing where he was leading me.

"Maybe they're all in there, including your brother, and they need our help."

Friends shouldn't make you feel guilty to get you to do something.

"Okay," I said. "I'll give it a try, but if this tunnel, if it *is* a tunnel, starts to collapse, then I'm out of here."

"Fine by me," said Jeff.

Maybe it wasn't good for me to believe in Jeff's dreams. He believed in them enough for both of us. He's also the type that gets it in his head to do something and he won't let go of it. He's like a dog with a bone.

We set down our demolition tools and picked up our candles. We cautiously started down the tunnel, which was about six feet high and another six feet across. The whole thing needed a good dusting. And it was more than slightly filled with cobwebs.

I like animals. But I don't particularly like spiders, and I'm sure I was walking into webs of some serious spiders that can kill you with a trace of their venom.

"Yuck," I said.

"Shhh," said Jeff.

"What do you mean 'shhh'?" I said. "I could die of a spider bite down here and you're worried about me being quiet."

"I don't want them to hear us coming," Jeff said.

I was embarrassed because I was usually the quiet one. Right then I stepped in water. The only thing I could think of was there might be an underground spring or something. It was deep enough to get my shoes wet.

"I think I see a light up ahead," said Jeff.

It was a soft green glowing light like those glow sticks you can get at Halloween.

"What is it?" I asked very quietly.

"I don't know," said Jeff.

We inched closer.

The glow spoke and I practically wet my pants.

"What's your name?" a sad little girl's voice said. It was coming from the green glowing light.

"Pardon me?" I said after a minute to collect myself.

"What's your name?" repeated the voice and now I could see her in the glow. She sounded so sad you could cry for her.

She was wearing a nightgown but it appeared that she and the glow were one thing.

"I think I'm going to puke," said Jeff.

"What's your name?" pleaded the girl.

"Becky," I said loudly but she didn't respond.

She said again, "What's your name?" and then she just sort of faded like a settling dust cloud.

"I think we just saw ourselves a ghost," said Jeff, "and we should now leave."

"There's no such thing," I said, "but don't ask me to prove it."

"I'm still shaking," said Jeff. "I'm turning around."

You know what? I was scared but I also knew I'd be even more scared if I turned and ran. I figured I had to go forward or I'd never be able to do anything again.

"Please help us!" we heard echoing from the end of the tunnel.

"Oh no," whined Jeff.

"Wait," I said, "I see another light."

"I see it too," affirmed Jeff.

"And it isn't glowing like the girl," I said, "look."

Jeff could see it too and it was a good thing. My candle was burning way down. The light we both saw looked like streaks of light coming from cracks through boards and it was right up ahead.

As my candle burned out I whispered, "If you're too scared . . ."

"I'm not," snapped Jeff, trying to act brave. "We have to go see who needs our help. We don't have a choice. If we see any more ghosts we'll turn back. Deal?"

"Maybe it wasn't a ghost. Maybe it was just some trick of the dark because our eyes aren't used to it," I suggested.

"That could be the stupidest thing I've ever heard of," said Jeff.

I decided to keep my mouth shut. Talking wasn't going to do any good. I should have told him that even though we got scared it didn't mean we had to get nasty with each other but I didn't.

We continued forward in silence. I heard the hissing noise very, very loudly. It was certainly an animal noise. It wasn't mechanical and it wasn't human. Then I heard crying and moaning.

The thing that truly scares me is someone being hurt. It sounded like something awful was being done to someone. I didn't like it one bit.

"Okay," I said, "let's turn around."

We stood there a second looking at the light and listening.

"Maybe we should take a look?" queried Jeff.

"Maybe," I said.

"Absolutely maybe," said Jeff.

10

Jeff blew his candle out and we shuffled our way toward the light. As we came closer to it, we could tell it was light from a room, leaking out through the slats of the boards.

"I'm sure it's an opening into their basement," whispered Jeff.

"Who is crying?" I asked quietly but I knew.

"I don't know," whispered Jeff.

We got closer and closer and the ground was getting muddier and muddier. I told Jeff to stop making those sucking noises with his feet when he pulled them up.

"I'm trying," he muttered.

"Shhh," I said.

We were right at the boards at the opposite end of the tunnel. The light was coming in through cracks between the planks and through a couple of knotholes. There was one knothole at just the right height for me to peek into the room. I looked

47

and I had to put my hand over my mouth to keep from shrieking.

At first I thought there was a dinosaur in the basement. There was a giant, chained lizard in the middle of this large room. It had to be at least ten feet long.

Over in the corner was the source of the crying. It looked like every kid in the neighborhood was behind bars, in a cage. The lizard looked like it was taking a rest.

I knew it wasn't a dinosaur. I'd seen that kind of lizard before but not in real life. I'd read about it and I'd seen a program on it. I was trying to remember.

"Look at that," whispered Jeff, "it's a Komodo dragon. They're like an endangered species."

"I knew that," I mumbled.

I was kind of irritated because I would have remembered it. However, I didn't have long to be mad. Suddenly, I couldn't see out of my knothole. It was as if it was going up or ... I was going down.

I was going down. I was sinking in the mud. I was now up to my knees.

"My shoes," I whispered, but with considerable alarm.

"I'm stuck. It must be quicksand," said Jeff, almost talking in normal tones.

"Be quiet," I demanded, "it's mud not quicksand."

"I still can't get out," said Jeff.

I thought he was going to cry. I grabbed onto anything to try to pull myself out. I reached out, sliding my hands all over the boards and getting a million splinters. Finally I felt something cold and metal close to the edge. It was a door latch, not a knob exactly, but some kind of door handle. I used it to pull on and got one leg out. I put my foot on a board next to the wall and then pulled my other leg out.

There was this loud pop as I pulled my leg free. I put it on the board next to my other foot so I was completely pressed against the wall. I carefully leaned my body over to look through the knothole, pressing all my weight against the wood to see if the dragon had woken up. I was still hanging onto the metal thing.

Something went "click."

To my complete surprise, the wall was a door and it swung out with me attached to it like a blood-sucking leech, right out into the room. It swung not just a little but all the way till it hit the wall. I tried not to breathe as I remained attached to it with my back to the dragon.

I slowly turned around. He was awake and looking at me.

"Hi," I said weakly.

The dragon lurched at me, pulling tight the chain that attached him to the wall. He then filled his neck and throat with air, making them look twice as big. Finally, he let out this incredibly ugly hiss that made me want to crawl to China.

"What did you do that for?" asked Jeff.

"I didn't do it on purpose," I said sharply.

"Now what?" he said.

I jumped off the door and went to pull Jeff out of the mud. He already had one leg out and so I bent over to help him pull the other leg out. My back was to the dragon. I heard something go "smack" and then something else hit the wall.

I whipped around while Jeff was saying, "Did you see that?"

Obviously I hadn't, but I saw that the dragon had turned and used his tail to send a chair flying across the room where it was broken to pieces against the wall. Jeff was free and he stood and unexpectedly grabbed my arm. I jumped twenty feet in the air.

"Don't ever do that," I said.

"Sorry," he said.

"Let's get out of here," I said.

"What about the kids in the cage?" said Jeff.

We heard a door open and someone start down the stairs.

"Later," I whispered, "let's get out of here for now."

We quickly grabbed the door handle, closing the door as quietly as we could, and then both of us hugged the door so we wouldn't get stuck in the mud again.

"There's no knob on the other side of the door," I whispered to Jeff.

"That's a good thing," he whispered back.

I looked through a crack in the door. There was the dark wizard, whatever he was, and he was talking to the dragon. It looked like the dragon was trying to bite him but he couldn't quite reach him.

"Hungry?" he said with an evil laugh. "We'll find you something to eat."

I noticed the kids had all moved to the back of the cage.

"And as for you," he said to the kids, "it won't be long now. I almost have everything together."

You want to know something weird? He may be evil but when I saw him this close I had to admit he was the best-looking man I'd ever seen. He looked like a model. He was dark and handsome with straight white teeth.

He was tapping on a book he was holding and laughing. He then turned, walked up the stairs, and shut the door. Both Jeff and I let out our breath. We had been holding it for what seemed like forever.

Without discussing it, Jeff lit his candle and we moved through the dark tunnel, bumping through every cobweb you could imagine but not caring. All I wanted to do was to get back to my own house where my mother was waiting.

51

11

Back at our end of the tunnel and upstairs, my mother wanted to show me a new tango routine she had made up.

"That's nice, Mom," I said, washing the mud out of my socks.

She danced away.

"Jeff," I said in exasperation, "what has happened to my parents?"

"It's all the adults," said Jeff. "They've gone wacko like the plants. They don't care about anything anymore. They're totally messed up."

Then the weirdest thing happened. It was like something in my heart exploded and rushed up into my throat and I couldn't hold it back. I didn't even know I was thinking about it. It hit all at once and I sobbed. I'd never sobbed in my life. I'd cried. I'd wept. This time I sobbed.

"They fed my dog to that dragon. I know they did. How could they do such a horrible, cruel thing?" I cried.

Jeff looked at me in shock. I know he'd seen me cry but this was a little more extreme.

"We don't know that," he said, trying to help.

"We don't know that they didn't," I wailed.

"Maybe dragons don't like beagles," said Jeff, again trying to make me feel hopeful.

"I know they do," I sniffed. "I know that Komodo dragons are carnivores. They eat other animals."

"Really," said Jeff. "You think he ate Tim?"

"Tim was an appetizer," I said, calming down one notch. "I'll show you."

We went upstairs and looked in the encyclopedia. I had to use the index because there wasn't an entry for Komodo in the K book. Komodo dragons were under Monitor, which is the name of the group of meat-eating lizards including the biggest lizard of all, the Komodo dragon.

"Look at this," I said, "they eat birds, mammals, fish . . . that means pets! Why don't they just say pets!"

"Why would someone eat Tim?" said Jeff, about to cry.

"Irving," I cried. "Poor Irving."

Jeff looked around the room, I think for a tissue for me and probably for himself but ended up offering me the corner of his shirt.

"Thanks but no thanks," I said, getting myself under control. I gave him the volume of the encyclopedia. "Here," I said, "I don't want to read anymore."

Jeff read slowly and then told me, "They grab their prey with their strong jaws and teeth and beat them against the ground. They are known to swallow small animals whole and I think I'm going to be sick."

I'm really not a screamer. I'm quiet, remember? I've always been quiet but I screamed.

Jeff jumped a foot. "What?"

"We've got to get those kids out," I shouted. "He's going to feed them to it next."

"No, it doesn't say anything in here about humans. They don't eat humans," said Jeff, wanting it to be true.

"We're mammals you fool," I said.

Jeff got all serious. "We have to rescue those other kids and avenge Tim's and Irving's death."

"You're being insane," I said. "You're going to be dancing the hula with my mother next. We can't get to that thing. What would we use?"

"Dynamite," he said. Then thinking more about it, "A hand grenade."

"I'll run out and buy one," I said, "just give me a few minutes to do my hair first. Don't be stupid. We don't have any weapons. . . . " Then it dawned on me. I continued, "We don't have any weapons except our minds. We can outsmart it."

"Now how are we going to do that?"

"Well," I pondered, "I guess I don't know yet, but it sounded good, didn't it?"

Jeff looked at me like I'd gone over the edge.

"What's our choice? Go in and try to beat it with a stick?" I said.

"I could go get my baseball bat," said Jeff.

That wasn't a bad idea just as a backup plan.

"I've got one," I said.

"Wait a minute," said Jeff. "Why did the wizards substitute our pets with the fake ones. Did they think we wouldn't notice?"

"I don't know," I said. "That Jeff is a very, very, good question." I thought some more. "We have to find out more about the wizards. We have to understand what they are up to and then we'll know how to get rid of the dragon and rescue the kids."

"Ya," said Jeff sarcastically, "that sounds simple. Do you want to go through the front door, the basement, or maybe we should just call them up?"

"Doberman or dragon," I said. "This isn't much of a choice."

"I thought you were good with animals," Jeff said.

"They have to want you to be good to them," I said.

"I say we go back into the basement. At least we can surprise him," said Jeff. "Oh yeah," he remembered, "even if we get past the Doberman and the dragon, we still have the wizards to face."

"I think I've seen one leave at night. He disappears out the back," I said.

"He just goes back inside," answered Jeff.

"Maybe not," I fired back, "maybe he has to leave for some reason."

"And maybe the tooth fairy will come and pull out all your teeth when you aren't looking, too," said Jeff.

I just sat silent.

"Okay, maybe you're right. Maybe that one won't be a problem and maybe we'll think of something," said Jeff. "Don't wizards use magic anyhow? Shouldn't we be thinking about that?"

"Precisely," I said like I knew what I was talking about.

It was starting to rain again.

"It'll be dark soon," said Jeff.

I spoke softly while my mother pounded a waltz on our now very out-of-tune piano, "We better get prepared."

12

"Y̲ou better go home and tell your mom you're going to be late," I told Jeff.

Jeff looked at me like I'd said something in a foreign language he'd never heard of.

He said, "She doesn't care what I do anymore. She almost forgets I exist except to ask me fifty times a day whether I like the way she's doing her hair. She spends the entire day looking in the mirror and brushing her hair different directions."

"What kind of spell do they have on people and why isn't it working on us?" I wondered out loud.

"Are we the only ones?" asked Jeff.

"Well who else isn't acting totally weird?" I stated.

"Uhhh," uttered Jeff. "I give up, maybe your brother?"

"Alex has always been strange, even before he got that gorilla suit. If he became stranger I doubt that we'd even notice it," I said.

"I didn't think you thought he was that weird,"

said Jeff surprised. "Because I always thought that gorilla thing was as weird as my Aunt Thelma's green tomato gelatin surprise."

"I still don't want you to trash him," I said.

"Fair," agreed Jeff.

"So I guess you're just staying here," I said, "you don't need to go home."

"Nope," said Jeff. "It takes too long anyway, and besides, I told you that something is out there."

"Well," I said, "let's go up to my room and watch out the window to see if one of them leaves."

We went upstairs, passing my mother in the hallway going, "One, two, cha, cha, cha. One, two, cha, cha, cha," all by herself. We waved at my dad lying on his bed staring at the television that no longer worked. He waved back but that was all.

We sat looking out my open window. I took the pruning shears, which I was keeping under my bed, and cut back enough of the foliage so we could have a hole to look out of.

"Not too much," said Jeff. "They'll see us."

"I'm not too worried," I told him. "If they can see us in the dark through all these leaves we are in serious trouble and hiding isn't going to help."

I got my binoculars and my mother's opera glasses. We sat and watched and waited.

Then the moon came out. We could see the moonlight on the house next door.

With the binoculars, it looked like the Doberman was sleeping on the front porch.

"Nice puppy," I said.

Jeff had to go to the bathroom.

"I'll be back," said Jeff, taking two birthday candles to get him there and back.

"You better," I said.

"You want anything?" Jeff asked.

"A pizza," I said.

"Ya," said Jeff, smacking his lips.

No sooner had he left the room than I looked out and sure enough there was the wizard man dressed in black flowing robes slipping out the side door and heading toward the back of the house. I shoved my head through the foliage to see him go out the back gate.

"Jeff," I whispered as loud as I could, "get back here."

He didn't hear me. I loaded up my backpack with the rest of the Christmas candles. I lit a skeleton candle from Halloween and started out the door.

I practically ran into Jeff coming around the corner. "Don't scare me like that," he snapped.

"Sorry," I apologized.

"Well, I didn't mean to yell at you," he said, "I guess I'm a little bit jumpy."

"Let's go," I said impatiently, "the wizard is out of there."

"Truly?" quizzed Jeff.

"Yes," I answered.

"Well," said Jeff.

"Well, let's go," I repeated.

We walked down to the basement slowly. Carefully we removed the boards we had laid against our side of the tunnel entrance.

"It's scarier at night," said Jeff.

"It's no darker," I said.

"Look," he said, pointing to the sides of the tunnel.

"What?" I asked.

"What are those, flecks of . . . gold?"

"Really?" I kind of shouted and shouldn't have. It slightly echoed down the tunnel.

We thought about scraping some of it off but then we realized that we just couldn't afford the diversion right then. We went straight to the end of the tunnel, peeked through, and to our significant relief, the dragon looked sound asleep. In fact, the kids in the cage were also asleep and someone was snoring something awful.

"I guess someone is allergic to Komodo dragons," I whispered.

"Ya," said Jeff, "me."

13

"They beat their prey to death by slapping them on the ground," Jeff repeated, wanting to make sure that I remembered what we were risking.

"I don't want to do this anymore than you do," I said. Then I had a sudden sinking feeling in my stomach like I'd just taken the express elevator from the top floor to the basement in three seconds flat.

"What's wrong?" said Jeff, sensing my enormous discomfort.

"Where'd the mud go," I said, barely audible.

"The mud?"

"Yes, the mud we were stuck in," I reminded him.

"Oh, that mud," he said.

We both lowered our candles to the ground where we saw dust where there had been mud before.

"It dried out," offered Jeff.

"Nice try," I said.

"So let's go back?" he said.

"What if this is a trap?" I thought out loud.

I answered myself and Jeff, "We don't have a choice."

Now you might think what we saw was odd (Jeff certainly did). If, however, the wizards could make deep mud change to dust in a small amount of time and cast a spell over the entire neighborhood, we could probably run as much as we wanted and we'd still have to face what they had in store for us.

"I think someone is messing with our heads," I whispered.

Right then a huge spider crawled on my arm. It was big enough to see in candlelight. I wanted to scream and brush it off, but I just brushed it off.

"What are you doing?" said Jeff impatiently.

"Brushing a spider off," I said, "this place is crawling with them."

"Let's get out of here, either going forward or back out, I don't care. Let's just do something," Jeff declared.

"Okay, be quiet," I whispered forcefully.

I blew out our candles and opened the door to the wizard's basement — or should I say dungeon. The wizards had rigged up one big sunlamp and the lizard was lying under it working on his tan, asleep, I hoped.

We tiptoed around the edge of the room toward the stairway. Some of the kids in the cage woke up and saw us. They started to talk and I held my fingers to my lips.

They screamed way too loudly, "Help!"

What did they think we had in mind, a picnic?

Jeff said, "Oh really," which I personally think was uncalled-for sarcasm even if we were highly stressed.

I nodded yes and made my way to the back of the cage where the door was. It had the biggest padlock I'd ever seen in my life. The key that fit it must have been three feet long.

I grabbed Jeff's arm and showed it to him. He just shook his head. I felt like we were scuba divers underwater. We were using hand signals and he was pointing upward like his tank was out of air.

Then the Komodo dragon decided to have a nightmare and whipped his tail against the cage, waking everyone up and causing them to start yelling and screaming.

"We'll be back," I said.

"Stay tuned," said Jeff, feeling for some reason that it was the time to try to be humorous, "we'll be right back."

A little girl I hardly knew was bawling and it broke my heart to leave her in that cage but we went up the stairs anyway. We didn't have to be quiet either because all the kids in the cage were still carrying on. We made it to the top of the stairs and opened the door.

The room we entered was dark with some light coming from a window and casting shadows on the wall. The door slammed behind us.

"Get the matches," I said, "we'll light the candles."

A flame appeared and I lit my candle.

"Where'd you get matches?" asked Jeff.

"You have them. You lit my candle," I said.

"No I didn't," he said with a frog, toad, and turtle in his throat.

Of course I tried to stay cool and not say, "Well who did then?" because I knew that would probably make me lose consciousness.

"Light your candle with mine," I said, trying my best to ignore what had happened.

Jeff lit his candle and there was now enough light to tell where we were. We were back in my bedroom.

"Maybe we took a wrong turn," said Jeff.

14

"Huh?" said Jeff out loud.

"This can't be my room," I said.

"I'm seriously confused," stated Jeff rather loudly.

"Shhh," I demanded. "Try the door again. The door we just came in. The one that leads to the basement."

"Oh," he said snidely, "that one. The one that leads to the hallway in your house."

He flung the door open.

"See," he said quite confidently and then when he realized his feet were well inside his mouth he sputtered, "it's the stairs to the basement."

"Someone is sure enough messing with our heads," I said and I'm telling you the truth I wasn't all that scared. I was intrigued.

"I guess I'll try another door?" asked Jeff.

I kind of laughed and said, "Ya, you never know what you're going to find in a closet."

He opened the closet door that looked like my

closet door and it led to the hallway in the wizard's house.

"You think there's more ghosts?" I asked.

"Hope not," mumbled Jeff, adding, "which way?"

"I don't know," I replied. "We have to go somewhere."

"I don't think we did enough planning before we came in here. We're looking for something and we don't know what it is or if it is even here," said Jeff.

"You're the one that had the dream," I reminded him.

"Don't get pushy about it. It was just a dream and you made a big deal out of it, not me."

"Whatever," I said.

I think we were arguing to avoid moving forward or even retreating. I suppose that's what arguing is for, when you don't want to move on, when you want to stay where you're at. I could hear a big old clock ticking somewhere. We moved toward the living room, following the sound.

There was nothing in the living room except the clock and for some reason we were drawn to it like a magnet. When we got up close enough to the face of the clock it suddenly chimed once, scaring us, and then quit working. By the way, it was a nice piece of furniture. My mother would've haggled an excellent price if it ever came up for sale at a garage sale.

"It stopped ticking," Jeff said.

"Let's keep moving," I said.

We left the living room and headed toward the front door entryway. The Doberman must have smelled us and was growling and scratching at the base of the door like he was trying to get through.

"Aw shut up," said Jeff, trying to sound tough.

"You'll just make him madder," I said.

He quit, however. He stopped growling.

"You were saying," said Jeff.

We turned and started up the stairs. The house was just like my dad had described it to me a long time ago. It was poorly constructed. The stairs were a hazard to anyone trying to walk up or down them. No two steps seemed the same.

"Sorry," I said to Jeff several times when I bumped into him.

"You're getting wax all over me," he said.

We reached the top, climbing the last step onto the landing, which was about the size of two normal steps. We stood there, looking down the second floor hall. I could feel a breeze so I tried to cover my candle and keep it from getting blown out. It didn't work.

It was as if the air went around my hand and snuffed the candle out. It also got Jeff's. We were in the pitch-dark again.

Someone or something whispered softly, "Out, out, brief candle."

"Did you say something?" asked Jeff. He was rummaging in his pockets for the matches. I could tell because I'd grabbed his arm.

"No," I answered, "I was hoping you'd said it."

"What is that?" said Jeff suddenly in a forced whisper.

I looked down the hall, assuming that was where he was focusing. At first I couldn't see anything and then I saw something forming in the dark. I tried to believe it was the moonlight coming through an open doorway. It was fluorescent and all misty like a swirling fog. It had kind of a pale bluish-green tint to it.

"What is that?" repeated Jeff.

"Something scary?" I ventured.

We stood and watched not knowing whether to run or not. The mist grew bigger till I'd say it was about the size of a man or woman and in some ways it looked like a person except most people aren't made of fluorescent bluish-green and yellow mist. It hovered there, kind of swirling around.

Then out of the mist came a piercing high-pitched scream that should've broken the windows. I dropped my candle and covered my ears. Then it was silent.

"Okay, I'm scared," said Jeff.

"No discussion on my part," I said with a quivering voice that betrayed my growing fear. Then, looking down the hall, I added softly, "Oh no."

The mist was traveling toward us at least

seventy-five miles per hour. There was no way to run away from it. I had just enough time to grab Jeff and push our bodies against the wall. I closed my eyes thinking I was a goner.

Whoever it was went by like ball lightning, bouncing off the ceiling, floor, and walls, and finally tumbling down the stairs. We were in the dark again but I felt this incredible cold feeling. I can only tell you that it felt like death. It felt like the coolness of a tomb.

"I'm freezing," said Jeff.

"Let's leave," I said.

"Which way?" asked Jeff. He sounded desperate.

He had a point. I wasn't exactly going to follow that thing down the stairs.

15

Just when you think things can't get worse, they often do. At first we thought we'd been saved. The lights in the house were turning on.

I thought they were an automatic thing, to keep burglars at bay. Then I realized that someone was turning the lights on and they were coming up the stairs.

"In here," I said as urgently as I could while still whispering.

I grabbed Jeff and pulled him through the door of a room right next to us. I shut the door as quietly as possible. While trying not to breathe, we listened as the footsteps coming up the stairs went past us and down the hall. A door opened clear down the hall and closed with a bang.

"Now what?" I thought out loud.

"We sneak down the stairs and get out of here," said Jeff.

"Don't be so loud," I cautioned. "We can't go out

the front door without fighting the Doberman and who knows if we can get by the dragon."

"We can't stay here," demanded Jeff.

"I know that," I said. "Let's at least take a look around before we leave. Light one of the candles. Maybe the key is in here."

"I don't want to," said Jeff.

"And why not?" I asked.

"Because, just because," replied Jeff.

"Give it to me," I said.

"Fine," pouted Jeff, "I'll do it. I'm not staying in here and if you take longer than twenty seconds, I'm leaving by myself."

"Fine," I shot back.

We lit one candle. I lifted it up and moved it slowly in front of us to show as much of the room as possible. We were in a bedroom.

It was done in dark, heavy-looking colors. In candlelight I could just tell that most of it was reddish, maybe burgundy. The bed was a four poster with curtains around it that were drawn shut. It made me think of Scrooge's bed in *A Christmas Carol*. I didn't want to think that because it made me think about ghosts and that was the last thing I needed to be reminded about.

"It's creepy," said Jeff.

"Well, that's candlelight. It always adds charm to a room," I said, trying to be uplifting.

"Let's get out of here," said Jeff, moving over

toward the window which was wide open. "Hey," he said, remembering the lights in the hallway, "how come they've got electricity and no one else does?"

"Good question," I said.

I went over next to the bed. On the nightstand was a small statue of Mozart. I could tell because I picked it up and it had his name on it. There was no alarm clock. There was a very old-looking book. I picked it up.

It had writing in it. I know, duh! However, it was handwritten like a diary.

"I think this is a journal or something," I told Jeff.

"I don't care," said Jeff. "Let's get out of here."

"All right, we can, just a minute, I have to look at something first," I spat out.

"Don't pull back those curtains," said Jeff.

It was too late. I did.

The good thing was I didn't scream. The bad thing was the old wizard, the one in the shimmering green and gold bathrobe, was lying on top of the covers and was probably dead.

"Is he breathing?" whispered Jeff.

"You check," I said very quietly.

"No way," he mouthed.

"Chicken," I whispered.

"Fine," he said and walked closer to him.

"Don't wake him up," I demanded.

"He's breathing. Are you happy?"

Suddenly, we heard a door shut loudly down the hall.

"What if the other one is coming in here?" Jeff said with a very hoarse, intense whisper.

"The closet," I mouthed.

We both scrambled as quietly as possible to the closet door only to find it locked. We both looked at the bed thinking about hiding under it. We simultaneously shook our heads to that idea.

"The window," we whispered in unison. It was wide open.

We're going to die, I thought to myself as we listened to footsteps getting closer to us from down the hall. They stopped every now and then as if to check something or to listen.

"I'm going for the trellis," said Jeff and he was out the window.

I quickly shoved the journal into my backpack, blew out my candle, and was right behind him.

"Will it hold both of us?" I asked as I climbed on and pressed myself as close to the house as possible.

"I sure hope so," said Jeff.

Jeff just finished his sentence when the door opened and someone walked in. Whoever it was turned on the lights and walked around the room. Jeff looked at me with wild panic in his eyes.

"What?" I mouthed.

He looked down. I thought he was afraid of heights or something. I was just going to tell him not to look down. However, I looked down.

There was the Doberman with his head cocked sideways, off his chain no less, staring up at us like we were the stupidest things he'd ever laid eyes on. He could've been correct.

"Jeez," I said under my breath.

The person in the room was rummaging through stuff. You could hear him moving things. It was like he was looking for something.

The man in the room said to the sleeping one, "Don't you look comfortable. I can't wait till I don't even have to see you. You thought you could control me, didn't you?"

Suddenly the trellis, which extended up another six or seven feet above us where it was attached, snapped. We looked at each other in holy terror and then both of us looked down at the dog, which was starting to growl.

"Just hang on," whispered Jeff, "don't move. Maybe it won't fall."

I swear to you on a stack of bibles that if he hadn't whispered the word "fall" with such force we would have been fine. However, we started falling away from the house just as the bottom six feet of the trellis snapped from our weight. I was doing my best not to scream or think about being in a body cast the rest of my life.

At first I thought we were going to break the

trellis into little tiny pieces and fall straight into the Doberman's jaws. We didn't. The trellis was actually quite strong in the middle and maybe the vine that was growing on it helped hold it together. We swung wide through the air like some circus act and I closed my eyes.

I felt a sharp jerk as the top of the trellis hit something. I let go, like a fool. I only fell about eight feet, which was enough to make my feet sting like crazy but I didn't break anything. The trellis had gotten hung up on a tree. We both fell through a bunch of branches to the ground.

My first thought was the whereabouts of the Doberman. I looked as hard as I could. He was trapped under the broken bottom of the trellis and was going crazy.

"Run," Jeff yelled at me.

For a second I looked back up toward the window. There was the dark wizard looking out the window down toward us.

16

I know he saw us and I know he knew it was us. I didn't know why he didn't just come get us. Who would've stopped him?

Jeff stayed over in Alex's room. I was worried about Alex. It dawned on me that he wasn't in the cage with the other kids. It was hard telling where he was. His gorilla suit was missing. My parents didn't care.

There was a big huge bunch of bananas on our front step in the morning. We didn't know where they came from. I thought of Alex as I ate four.

I was exhausted because I had spent half the night reading the journal by candlelight and the other half waiting for the other wizard to come get me. The journal was hard to read. It jumped all over the place with two different sets of bad handwriting.

At first it was almost like a cookbook. There were formulas of chemicals to boil and notes about turning a frying pan into gold. I thought that might be quite attractive but not very practical. You couldn't cook with it and you couldn't wear it. What would you do with it? Would you hang it on the kitchen wall until someone broke in and stole it? Seems a waste of time and energy to me.

Then there were plant experiments, which I assumed was where our jungle came from. There were seven whole pages on creating a lush landscape out of a normal landscape. I wish I could've deciphered everything it said, but I couldn't. I picked up words like *speeding up the vibration of certain common plants through the use of speech*, but then there was just one page where the handwriting changed and in bold letters that dug in the page was written, *jungle*.

There were two different handwritings like that all the way through. The one was kind of scribbly but you could make it out and the other was mean-looking. I figured it was the old wizard and the other one alternating. It seemed as though the old one would start something and it was sort of a good thing, but then the other one would come in and take over and make it bad.

The subjects changed, too. At first he was writing about experiments and then by the middle of the journal the heavy handwriting was going on and on about power. It was power this and power that. Most of the time it was about how powerful he was becoming and the power he had over plants, animals, and people. He was even boasting of having power over the weather.

At one point the old wizard's handwriting was talking about the positive power of animals and their instincts but it stopped and the heavy handwriting wrote, *Tell me!* The next two pages looked as though they had been ripped out.

I kept flipping ahead trying to figure it out and was really shocked by the last entries in the diary. The dark one was doing an experiment. There were a couple of pages of formulas that looked like something out of an advanced algebra textbook in the severely heavy handwriting: *I have the power to destroy and I will because I can at the next full moon. He can't stop me even though he tries. He sleeps and I'm awake.*

Then there was an entry from the nicer handwriting. *All wrong. Has to be stopped. Power seeks only more of itself.*

The last thing written in the journal was the nice handwriting, *I don't know how long I can keep Jeff and Becky safe. I need them to help. I don't know if they destroy him whether I'll be destroyed, too.*

Then at the bottom of the page was *I am a brother to dragons and a companion to owls. Job 30:29.*

I was tired of waiting and I went and got Jeff up. My mother had been up for hours singing and trying to get me to come down and square-dance with her.

"Thank you for asking," said Jeff politely when she asked him to join her, "but I usually don't do much square dancing before breakfast."

My mother didn't care. She just said, "A do-si-do and away I go," and went dancing off into the other parts of the house.

Jeff ate bananas.

"Know what I think?" I said.

"I never know what you could be thinking," said Jeff, "and most of the time, I don't want to know."

"You'll want to know this time, because it just so happens to include the fate of the world as we know it, and at the least our own personal destruction by the evil wizard who is living next door."

"How do you know?" asked Jeff, not believing at all.

"I read it all night in his journal," I declared. "How else?"

"Okay, okay," agreed Jeff, "what did he say?"

"First, how close do you think we are to a full moon?"

"Wow, I'd say we were there. It looked pretty full last night. Maybe it will be at its peak tonight then," said Jeff.

"That's what I was afraid of," I said. "You know what that means?"

"We won't need to use so many candles?" said Jeff.

"No, we have to go back into that house imme-diately," I said.

"I don't think so," said Jeff, using the tone of voice our teachers usually used when they talked about . . . responsibility. "In fact, I've had time to think about it and I think those kids should take responsibility for getting themselves into that mess and they should find their own way out of it. How else are they going to learn to be responsible?"

I said, "What happened to being responsible to help people who need help."

"I was just kidding," Jeff said, though he wasn't. "But I still don't want to go into that house."

"Here," I said, shoving the pages in his face where we were the subject.

"Why didn't my dad let me move to Alaska with him?" said Jeff.

17

Jeff spent the morning figuring out if it was the full moon or not. He was trying to figure out how many days it had been since we became the jungle. I decided it didn't matter. We had to stop the evil wizard sometime, it might as well be today.

I had figured the two men in the diary were the old man and the young one and it wasn't hard to figure out who was who. I didn't know why they were writing in the same diary.

"It's almost like they are the opposite of each other," I said to Jeff.

"Maybe they are brothers or something, or partners and one of them is good and the other is bad," reasoned Jeff.

"I think the old one is trying to stop the bad one," I said. "I think he is the reason we haven't been caught by the bad one and put in the cage with the rest of the kids."

"What makes you think that?" Jeff said.

I just looked at him.

"Oh no," he said, "it's one of those things you know?"

"I don't know for sure," I said. "I only have a feeling and look what he wrote about us."

"So what are we going to do?" asked Jeff.

"First, we're going to wait till it is dark. Then we're going to go back through the basement with bolt cutters and get the kids out and then — "

Jeff interrupted me, "You really think he's going to destroy us?"

"Yes," I said bluntly.

We looked all over our garage for the bolt cutters. I knew we had some. We found them and then we had to take some steel wool and clean the rust off and then put some oil on them.

"They'll work," I said.

"We better try them," said Jeff as he wrecked my bicycle lock.

"They work," I said, holding up my broken lock.

"Uh, sorry," said Jeff.

"We need more candles," I said.

I went in and asked my mother, who had moved on to practicing Israeli folk dances.

"You're losing weight, Mom," I said.

She didn't answer me.

"Mom?!" I screamed.

She stopped and looked around the room. Suddenly she saw me. It was weird because it was like a cloud lifted for a second.

"Becky," she said tenderly, then back went the cloud and she was goofy again dancing around the room.

"Mom," I screamed this time, "do we have any emergency candles?"

"In the basement above the freezer in a box, two, three, kick," she answered from somewhere far away where people only dance through life.

I went downstairs which, even though it was daytime, was dark. I felt around for the freezer and found a box on a shelf above it. I pulled it off and drug it upstairs. She was right. There were several emergency candles and, get this, a flare!

"Now we're talking," said Jeff.

Something large flew or swung or swooped past the kitchen window. Of course the window was covered by leaves so we couldn't really see, but it was large.

"What was that?" I said.

"I don't think we want to know," said Jeff.

We stepped outside using the shears to cut the undergrowth that had grown in the night. There was no one there that we could see.

"Whatever it is, it's gone," I said.

"It was big, wasn't it?" Jeff said. "Do you think it was Alex?"

I told him, "I don't know."

We had our candles. We had our flare. We had our bolt cutters. Now we had to wait for the moon.

"Why wait?" asked Jeff.

I reminded him that the man was going to be busy destroying us and it would be a nice diversion so we could get the kids out.

"We'll tell them to get their parents and get out through the jungle."

"They'll get lost," said Jeff matter-of-factly.

"They're lost now," I told him. I knew it wasn't a great plan. It was, at least, a plan.

We sat and waited. We went upstairs and crawled out onto the roof on the opposite side of the house from the spook house. That way my mother couldn't drive us crazy with her dancing. She was doing ballet in the afternoon.

I was looking at the journal again. I noticed that on the last page there was a line that had been written in pencil and then erased. You could still feel the indentation where the words had been. I stepped back into the house and using a pencil I shaded very lightly where the words had been erased. Where I shaded appeared words.

It said, *Love may be the only antidote to power.*

"What's an antidote?" asked Jeff.

"It's like when you take poison, it keeps you from being killed by it."

"That's a good thing," said Jeff.

18

I heard an owl. I got the binoculars and looked out. I couldn't see anything. I looked on the porch. I couldn't see the Doberman anywhere.

"Quick, let's move. I don't think he's there," I said to Jeff.

"And where is he then?" he insisted.

"How should I know?" I said, wondering why I had to have all the answers. "Let's just get moving."

"Whatever," said Jeff.

We went outside. The moon was shining on the wizard's house. We went over to where we could crawl under the fence. I got my pack caught on the fence and Jeff wanted to use the bolt cutters to get it loose.

"I don't think so," I told him.

I easily pulled it free. We ran up to the house like military commandos, low to the ground. We were at the front door and ready to go in. Jeff got cold feet.

"Doesn't look like anyone's home," he said.

An owl hooted.

"I'm scared, too. We can be scared together. I don't know what's going to happen," I told him.

We held hands, which was weird on top of weird. The door was unlocked. Jeff opened the door and I went in first. We dropped hands and I turned on the light switch.

I walked over to the stairs.

"Where are you going?" asked Jeff.

"I have to take the book back," I said.

"Are you kidding me?"

"I can't keep it," I explained, "that would be stealing."

"Well, what do you think this is? A library? We're going to be destroyed and you want to do the honest thing?" Jeff asked me, totally puzzled.

"If I die, I don't want one of the last things I did to be stealing this book! Now you're either honest or you're not."

"How about breaking and entering to return it?" asked Jeff.

I thought for a moment. He did have a certain logic to his question.

I said, "Two wrongs don't make a right."

"You're weird," said Jeff.

I headed up the stairs.

"What if you meet that misty lady thing?" he asked.

"Don't remind me," I said and kept walking.

86

"What am I supposed to do?" said Jeff.

"Wait for me," I said.

In two seconds flat he was up the stairs and beside me.

"I think we should stick together," said Jeff.

There seemed to be no one in the house. We went to the second floor. I flipped the hall light on and went over to the room we had been in the night before. Carefully I opened the door.

I flipped on the light and I screamed. I screamed because this time the curtains on the bed were pulled back and the dark wizard was lying on the bed fast asleep. My scream could've woken the dead and he didn't budge.

"We're dead," said Jeff.

"He's dead," I said, going over closer to the bed.

"No he isn't," said Jeff. "His chest is moving."

"Why didn't he wake up when I screamed?" I whispered.

"Why are you whispering?" said Jeff.

"I don't know," I whispered again.

"What do they do?" questioned Jeff. "Take turns sleeping? Like they only have one bedroom in this house. It's crazy. Turn off the light and let's get out of here."

"Don't have to tell me twice," I said.

I took the journal out of my pack and placed it back by the side of the bed.

"Let's go," I said.

We turned off the lights, quietly shut the door,

and then went gangbusters down the hallway and the stairs till we made it to the ground floor.

"Now what?" said Jeff.

"We rescue the kids," I whispered, and then added in a loud voice, "we're leaving now and we won't be back."

Jeff looked at me like I was totally nuts, especially when I went and slammed the front door but stayed inside.

"It's a diversionary tactic," I muttered.

We tiptoed toward the kitchen and the basement stairs. I opened the kitchen door in a flood of light. There standing, well, maybe floating in the middle of the floor, was the old wizard in his shimmering gold and green robes and his pointy hat.

19

The kitchen lights were off. The brilliant light in the room was coming from an intense light around the wizard.

"You have to destroy the circle in the attic," said the wizard in a voice so deep that it vibrated everything in the room.

"How?" I managed to spit out even though my mouth was suddenly drier than the desert.

"Destroy it or it will destroy everything," he said, and then like a lightbulb being turned off he vanished and we were left in darkness.

We stood still, there in the dark, waiting for something to happen.

I heard his voice again, this time softly, "I can't protect you anymore."

It was quiet again and I reached over and felt for the kitchen light. I turned it on. The room really was a kitchen this time.

"Do we go get the kids free or save the world first?" I asked Jeff.

"Is this a trick question?" he asked. "How about none of the above?"

"Not much use saving them if everything is destroyed, is there?"

"Guess not," Jeff said reluctantly.

"Well," I said, "let's go."

"We don't know what we're doing," said Jeff.

"I guess we'll know when we get there," I said quite heroically but I didn't mean a word of what I said. I felt like I was living in a dream and someone else was talking, not me.

We left the kitchen and as we turned on the lights and climbed the stairs I heard the owl calling and then I swear it switched in mid-hoot into the Doberman barking. It sounded like it was somewhere in the house, maybe in the kitchen.

"Run," said Jeff.

We ran as quietly as we could to the second floor.

"I have to check something," I said.

I went over to the bedroom door where I'd found the journal. I carefully opened the door and turned on the light. The dark evil wizard wasn't there. In his place on the bed was the old wizard and he was fast asleep.

I turned off the light and closed the door.

"They are the same person," I said. "Only one of them is awake at a time."

"Huh?"

"Doesn't it make sense," I said, "when the owl is

out, the old man is there, and when the Doberman is out, the dark evil one is awake. It all makes sense."

"To you maybe," Jeff said stunned and then it clicked with him. "Maybe you're right. We've never seen the two together. How do they do that?"

"Who knows?" I said.

We paused, knowing that the attic was next. We walked back to the stairs with nothing but dread. We were two kids without a choice.

There was a rumble above us as we heard something being dragged across the floor. Then there was the hiss.

We looked at each other in terror.

"Huh?" we said together.

"Jinx," I added, but it wasn't funny.

We slowly went up the stairs to the attic.

The door was open.

"Well look who is here," said the dark wizard, standing at the far side of a room that looked bigger than it should have been if you looked at the outside of the house. "Should I add that I've been waiting for you?"

The windows were all open and you could smell the outside jungle air and something else. It was a strange smell, like a combination of sweet things and bitter things. Then I realized he was burning incense in a large pot in a corner of the room.

In the middle of the room, chained to a post, was

91

the dragon. He looked so pathetic and I felt sorry for him, even though he probably ate Irving.

Poor Irving, I thought.

Then I thought I was hearing my heart beating and then I thought I was hearing Jeff's heart beating, but then I realized that it was a beating sound that was coming from the entire room.

"Nice to finally meet formally," said the wizard, "don't you think?"

"I'm not sure," I said.

"Maybe we should go," said Jeff, "you look kind of busy."

"Oh I am," said the wizard with a very evil laugh and the door slammed shut behind us.

Instinctively we turned and tried to open it. It was locked.

"I suppose you're wondering why you aren't locked up in the cage with the rest of the scum," said the wizard.

Then I felt the strangest thing. It was like a magnet pulling me or a tractor beam. I, well, and Jeff too, were being pulled closer to the dragon.

"No," I screamed and the dragon lifted his head toward me and shot out his tongue.

"Lovely little pet, isn't he? Oh, don't worry," the wizard said, "I won't let him eat you . . . yet."

"Why are you doing this?" I yelled at him and the magnetic pull or whatever it was stopped, however, my feet were stuck where they were. I couldn't move. I could've been a mannequin.

"Now that's a good question," he said, sitting down on a wooden stool on the other side of the dragon from us. "It's kind of complicated," he continued, "and really all that matters is that I'm going to destroy this little piece of the world tonight and you're not going to stand in my way and anything the old man told you won't stop me."

His whole face and voice changed to almost a growl as he added, "I don't need him."

Buy some time, I thought to myself, ask questions.

"Who is he?"

"Oh wouldn't you like to know," he said. "Why he picked you two to protect, I have no idea. You seem quite inferior to me. Now, however, you may prove useful."

"What do you mean?" said Jeff, sounding quite tough if you ask me.

"However," he said, looking at Jeff, "I don't need you."

He flung his hand in the air like he was batting at a fly and right before my eyes Jeff disappeared.

I've never been so sure in my life that something really bad was about to happen.

"Don't," I pleaded.

20

"**P**lease don't hurt Jeff," I begged.

"Oh relax," said the wizard, "he'll hurt himself if I don't."

Then he stared at me hard and I felt like he was reading my thoughts.

"You think you know things, don't you?" he said, looking intensely at me with his black eyes.

"I don't know," I said.

"You knew I was a wizard when I first moved in," he said.

Destroy the circle, I heard the old wizard in my head.

"What?" I said out loud.

"You hear things, too?" said the dark wizard.

"No," I said sharply.

I thought, *what circle?*

"You know he put protection on you. You know I can't destroy you . . . but it's wearing off. I can feel it."

I didn't know if he was fooling me or testing me or what. I wondered if I should tell the truth or just play along.

"I don't know what you're talking about." My throat sounded funny.

"Oh, isn't that too much. You know you're in league with him. Don't lie. Tell me what he told you."

"Nothing," I said. "I don't know what you're talking about."

It looked like he was trying really hard to read my mind again. He put both hands to his head like he had a migraine and might throw up.

"Oh, he's blocked all thoughts about himself from me. I'll get him anyway," he yelled.

The moon was starting to appear through a hole in the roof. We both looked up.

"Ahhh," said the wizard. "It is almost time."

Stall him, was the only thing I could think.

"Who is the old guy?" I asked again. "Why do you hate him?"

"Who cares?" he chided. "Don't you know? I thought you knew everything. Well, let's just say I'm his worst nightmare and he's mine. He didn't know what to do with his power. He was content to make flowers grow bigger. He needed me to give him some vision. What he didn't know was that I was much stronger than he," said the wizard, going about his preparations at a table actu-

95

ally quite close to the dragon, who was pulling on his chain.

I thought, *He's going to pull the house down.*

"I hate weakness," he mumbled to himself.

"Excuse me?" I said. "Were you talking to me?"

"Shut up," said the wizard.

Right then the moon looked full above us and filled the room with its eerie blue glow.

"Now, we're going to have some fun," said the wizard.

"What are you going to do?" I asked.

"Wouldn't you like to know. Be quiet."

"I think I have a right, seeing how I'm part of this," I said.

"Hmmmm, I see why he picked you. You keep your head even though you're scared. It's a good trait. Too bad you won't be using it anymore," he laughed.

"I don't think it is nice to intentionally frighten people," I said.

"You don't?" laughed the wizard. "It's hysterical."

"Why?"

"Why not?" he answered me. "That is the answer to all your questions. Why not? I'm going to destroy not all the world but a big chunk, and why? Why not? Because something has to die in order for it all to be reborn. Don't you get it?" he raised his voice. "I'm changing everything because I can."

"What did you do with my dog? Why did you turn him into plastic?" I yelled at him.

"Oh, get off the pets. He did that. He turned your precious doggie into plastic to keep him from being a dragon snack. He hid them from me. It was his idea of a joke. Not funny at all if you ask me."

He took a sack of something and started pouring a white powder on the floor in a large circle around the dragon. It was making me sneeze and it smelled funny, like bad compost or something.

He finished and I felt myself being lifted off the floor. I was floating across the room and into the circle where he put me down. I still couldn't move. I was frozen into an upright position.

He was petting the dragon.

"Nice dragon," he said.

The dragon actually liked it. I hoped he'd bite him. The wizard opened a book and started reading.

"Eye of newt," he looked at me laughing, "just kidding." He continued in a deep loud voice, "The dragon who is our friend, and a child whose innocence will now end, that's you," he nodded toward me, "and now this circle where power comes and death and life join and the beginning becomes the end and the end becomes the beginning. . . ."

I heard thunder, and it hit me that he was talking about me and death in the same sentence and I might really die.

He continued mumbling, now in a foreign language. I thought about Irving, and Jeff, and my parents, and all my friends, and Alex, whom I hadn't seen forever, and I missed everyone. I was homesick like I was at camp too long. Pretty soon, I felt tears running down my cheeks and I thought about my mom doing the cha-cha and it made me cry harder. I loved her. I loved her dancing and the stuff she bought at yard sales and I loved my dad and I even loved Alex's gorilla suit.

Then I started crying like a faucet had been turned on.

"No crying," he screamed at me. "You stop or I'll destroy you."

He just scared me more and I cried harder. He was rushing over to me with a rag.

"Don't let them touch the ground!" he demanded.

"What?" I wailed. "I want my mom and my dad and my brother and my Irving!"

Right then, before he could shove that dirty rag in my face, a tear dropped to the ground and I watched as it traveled and hit the powder that outlined the circle and it started consuming it like acid. My one tear was eating up the circle. There was smoke everywhere and in five seconds flat the circle was gone.

"You idiot!" the wizard howled.

21

Then a cloud went over the moon.
"No!" shrieked the wizard and suddenly I heard the owl hoot.

I looked over and where the evil wizard had been, in a heap on the ground, was the old wizard. Then I realized I could move. I got away from the dragon and ran toward the old man. It was the wrong move to make.

The dragon was now freaked out, and jerking the chain, it pulled the post to the side.

"Stop it," I said to it.

It pulled its neck back to lunge again. I put my hands over my head to wait for the ceiling to collapse. My eyes were closed.

I heard a huge crash like glass breaking. I opened my eyes and there was my brother Alex in a pair of leopard-skin shorts, with a clear complexion and clean hair. He was tan and muscular and was standing in the middle of the room.

"Jeez," I said.

The lizard was kind of shocked, too.

"We have to get out," demanded Alex.

"Okay," I said, "but there are kids in the basement."

"You, me, we try," he said. "Come," and he motioned toward the window.

"How about the stairs?" I said as the post where the dragon was chained creaked a huge creak.

"Now," said Alex, grabbing me around the waist and jumping with me out the window.

"The wizard . . . !" I screamed as the post broke and the attic ceiling collapsed.

Alex had grabbed a vine and we were swinging through the trees.

"Hang on," he said as we jumped to another vine.

In a landing that would make a pilot proud, we stopped on the ground next to our house.

"Where did you learn to do that?" I yelled enthusiastically but Alex was gone. He'd grabbed another vine and was swinging into the jungle.

I turned to look at the haunted house. I watched in the moonlight as it collapsed until there was just a pile of rubble on the ground.

I shed another tear thinking that the kids in the basement, including Jeff, were buried.

Right then, from out of the jungle, I saw a flare.

"Who is it?" I said, picking up a stick to fight them if I had to.

"It's me," said Jeff.

"What?" I yelled, not believing it could be true.

"And I got the kids out of the basement," he said.

"How?" I said, hugging him.

He said, "He put me down there with the bolt cutters still in my backpack. I thought you were killed in the attic. I was coming up to get you when the house started to crumble."

I hugged him again in front of everyone. The kids looked wiped. They acted like they didn't know who they were or where they were. Then there was an incredible explosion that sent fireworks soaring above the trees like the Fourth of July. The blast threw us all to the ground. I couldn't hear or even see for several minutes.

When I stood up, I looked over toward the wizard's house. It was gone completely. There was no debris. It was gone like it had never been there.

We ran to my porch. I screamed for joy. The real live Irving was there. Irving, my precious dog, was home and I was so happy to see him. He was sitting on the couch looking at me like he'd been there all the time and I was a complete fool for making a fuss about him.

22

It took about three weeks but the vegetation on our block went back to normal. It was better than before somehow, but it wasn't at all a jungle. The street was back. The sidewalks were back. The power was back on. Everything including our parents seemed normal, like nothing had happened.

In fact, sometimes I wonder if anything really did happen that summer. Jeff and I seem to be the only ones who remember anything about the wizards and even the house next door. My parents don't remember a thing.

"You must've had a dream," my mother said.

"No, I didn't," I said to Jeff.

"Don't tell me," he said. "I was there and we should've gotten the gold in the tunnel."

I felt sorry for the old wizard, not the mean one. I wondered if he had been killed in the explosion. I also felt sick about the dragon. He didn't really mean anyone any harm. He was just being himself.

Then one night, I woke in a cold sweat. I heard an owl and it was right outside my window. I got up and cautiously looked outside. I couldn't see anything. Then the next morning, I went outside and there on the front porch was the Doberman with a pink bow around his neck and a note in his mouth.

Thanks for all the help, it said. *Would you take care of this young man and give him a name? P.S. The dragon and I are fine.*

My parents weren't thrilled with my gift but what do you do? I told them we had to keep him till the real owner came back and they bought it. I guessed the dog was now mine. He's a whole lot nicer than before. He's downright lovable. Irving even likes him. I called him Sweetie because he likes cookies so much.

I started to worry about Alex but my parents didn't seem too concerned. He was missing for quite awhile. In fact, he was still not around and it was almost time for school to start.

Then one day I was coming home from swimming in the pool and I saw Alex's gorilla suit and his leopard-skin shorts hanging on the clothesline. He was in the house eating cornflakes like a normal person, reading a book.

"Hi Alex," I said.

"Hi," he said, carefully looking up from his book. He was reading, *How to Be a Wiz at Everything*.

Then he winked at me.

No Bake Cookies

You get out a pot and you put 2 cups of sugar in it. Then you put $\frac{1}{2}$ cup of butter or margarine, $\frac{1}{2}$ cup of milk, and 2 tablespoons of powdered cocoa in it. Now before you do anything else you take a bowl and you put 3 cups of quick oats in it, $\frac{3}{4}$ cup of coconut, $\frac{1}{2}$ cup of nuts, and $\frac{3}{4}$ cup of those little marshmallows. You mix that all up.

Now you can turn the heat on the pan (get an adult's permission first), stir it, bring it to a boil, and after it boils, you let it boil for 1 minute. Then you pour that mixture over the stuff in the bowl and mix it up. Then you just take a spoon and put the cookie-size drops of it on some waxed paper, Let that cool and you've got yourself some No Bake Cookies.